Look Out, Jack! The Giant Is Back!

by Tom Birdseye

illustrated by Will Hillenbrand

Holiday House / New York

Last you heard of Jack, he had outsmarted the fee-fi-fo-fum giant and made off with the bags of coins, the hen that laid golden eggs, and the magic harp that could sing so pretty. That old giant lay dead at the bottom of the beanstalk. So you thought that was the happily-ever-after end of that.

Right?

Wrong!

Not more than ten minutes later, the dead giant's big brother showed up. He was something fearful, twice the size of the little one, ten times as nasty, and as ugly as slug pie. He started tying a rope ladder together so he could climb down and get Jack for what he'd done.

Lickety-split, Jack and his mama packed up the coins and the hen and the harp, then hopped on a boat to America, where Jack bought a nice little farm in the mountains of North Carolina.

"That old giant will *never* find us here!" Jack said, and settled down to raising the prettiest prize-winning roses you've ever seen. Life was good, and peaceful, and oh-so fragrant...

...until one day in August when it was so hot Jack had to pack the hen in ice to keep her from laying hard-boiled eggs instead of golden ones. He'd just finished the job and was having some lemonade on the front porch, when there boomed a deep, angry, thundercloud of a voice.

Wham blam hickity hack!
I'm gonna get that boy named Jack!
He now be living, but soon he'll roast!
I'll spread him with mustard and eat him on toast!

"Uh-oh,"
said Jack.

Uh-oh was right. Standing there atop a mountain, glaring down at him with mean green eyes, was you-know-who.

"Give me the money, Jack!" the giant demanded. "And the hen and the harp, too! Bring 'em to me now, or I'm comin' down to get 'em and it won't be pretty!"

Jack looked around. No chance of running for it. He was caught red-handed. Which would have made most folks as nervous as a duck in the desert.

Not Jack, though. He waved real friendly-like and hollered, "Be right there, Mr. Giant!"

Then right quick he and his mama put together a little picnic for the occasion: three hundred seventy-three platters of Southern fried chicken; six hundred pounds of mashed potatoes with gravy; huge heaps of boiled okra, fried green tomatoes, and coleslaw; one thousand biscuits with sweet cream butter and strawberry jam; ninety-nine gallons of tart apple cider; a red-checked tablecloth to spread everything on; and a dozen of his finest, most fragrant long-stemmed roses for a centerpiece.

All of this—plus the coins, the hen, and the harp—
Jack packed onto his two mules, Thistle and Thorn. Then
up the path he went, whistling like he didn't have a trouble
in the world. Because, you see, Jack—being as smart as a
tree full of owls—had a plan.

As soon as Jack got to the top of the mountain,
the giant started in again:

Wham blam hickity hack!
I'm gonna get that boy named Jack!
He now be living, but soon he'll roast!
I'll spread him with mustard and eat him on toast!

Then the giant stood back with an evil, gap-toothed grin, waiting for Jack to fall all over himself trembling in fear.

But Jack smiled and said, "Nice to meet you, too, Mr. G.!"

"Maybe you didn't hear me right," the giant grumbled. He shouted so loud windows rattled clear up in New York City:

Wham blam hickity hack!
I'm gonna get that boy named Jack!
He now be living, but soon he'll roast!
I'll spread him with mustard and eat him on toast!

As calmly as you please, Jack said, "I figured you to be hungry."
He pulled out a platter of that Southern fried chicken and waved it
in the mountain breeze so the giant could get a good whiff. "Think
of it as an appetizer," he said, "to have before you eat me on toast."

Insulted that Jack wasn't responding to his show of ferocity, the giant
snatched the chicken out of Jack's hand and shoved it, platter and all,
down his throat in one bite.

Jack said, "By all means, help yourself." He was busy spreading the rest
of the picnic goodies out on the red-checked tablecloth. "But tell me,
where do you think I should put the roses?"

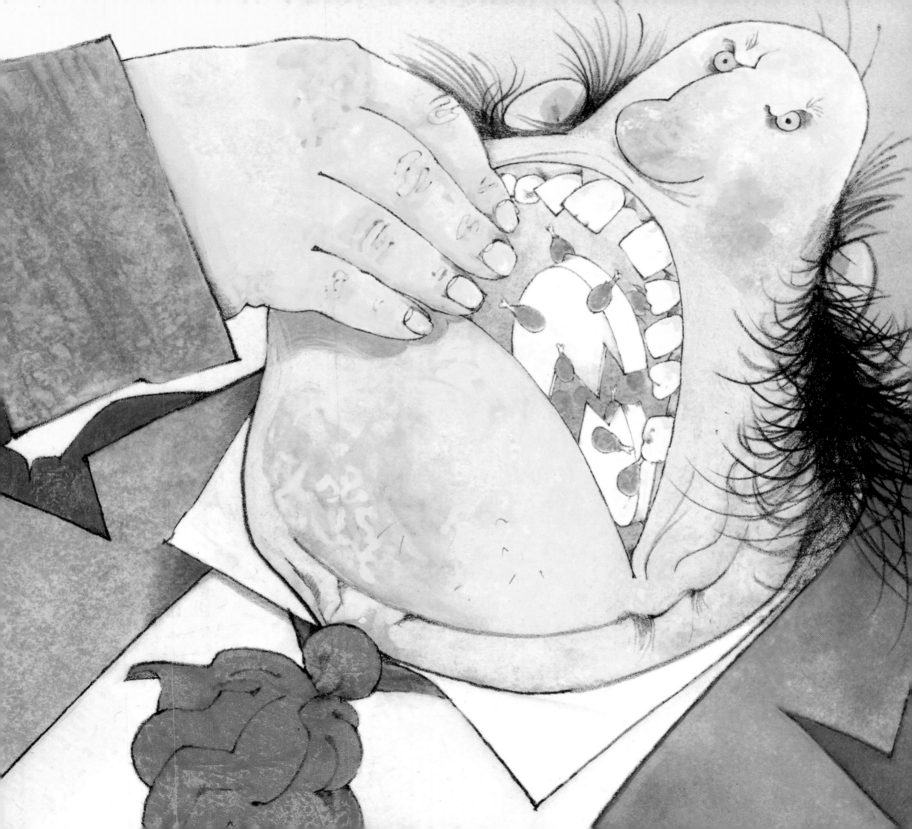

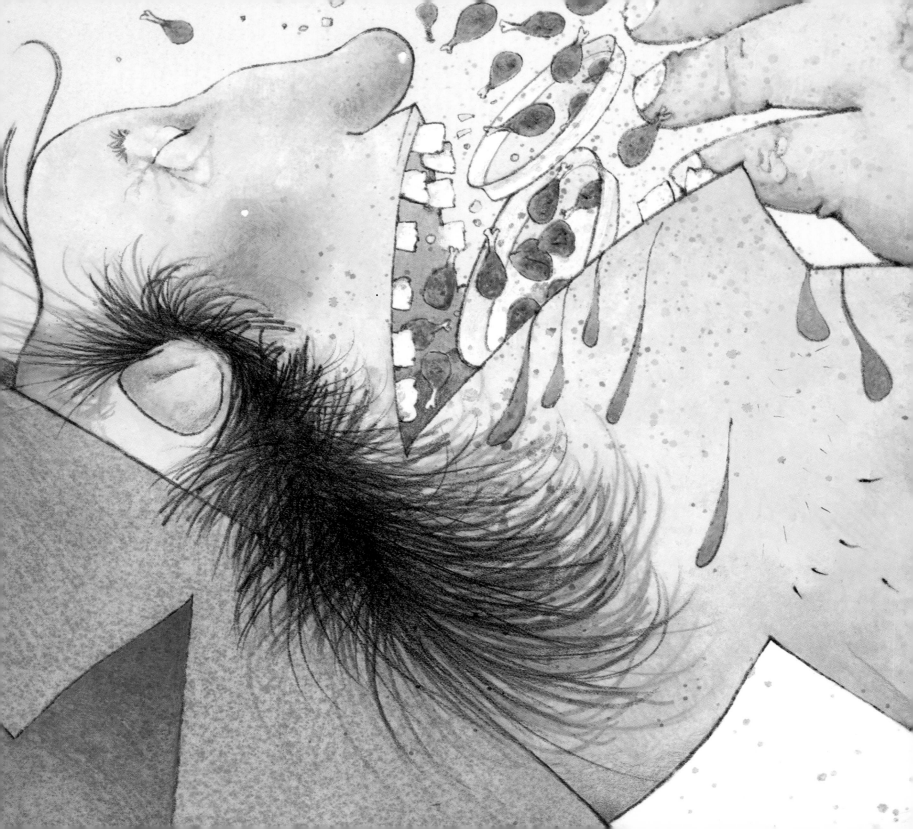

"ROSES?" The giant couldn't stand it. Just what did he have to do to get some respect? He snapped down another platter of fried chicken. Then another. And another. (He'd show Jack a thing or two!) Until all three hundred seventy-three were gone. And the six hundred pounds of mashed potatoes with gravy. And the huge heaps of boiled okra, fried green tomatoes, and coleslaw. And the one thousand biscuits with sweet cream butter and strawberry jam. And even the red-checked tablecloth! Then he washed it all down with those ninety-nine gallons of tart apple cider.

"So there!" the giant bellowed after the last gulp. He began again:
"Wham blam hickity hack!" But quickly his volume faded.
"I'm gonna get that boy named…" His stomach was starting to feel
a right might uncomfortable from all that food he'd crammed in.
It was too much, even for a giant.

"Aw, you get the point, Jack," the giant moaned. "But before I eat
you, where's the money?"

"Oh, yeah," Jack said. "Sorry. I almost forgot." He hauled out the
bags of coins. "Here they be, Mr. G."

The giant's belly began to rumble and gurgle in a disturbing way.
His next words came out with hiccups in between. "And the—HICCUP—
hen that lays golden eggs. Did you bring the—HICCUP—hen, Jack?"

"Why, sure," said Jack. He held up the hen and gave it a little peck of a kiss.

The giant belched so big—BURRRRRRP!—folks in the valley thought a thunderstorm was brewing. "And the magic harp," he said with a grimace. "I want to hear the harp sing."

"Good idea," said Jack, reaching for the harp. "Nothing like the right song to calm an upset stomach."

"What song do you wish, Master Jack?" the harp asked.

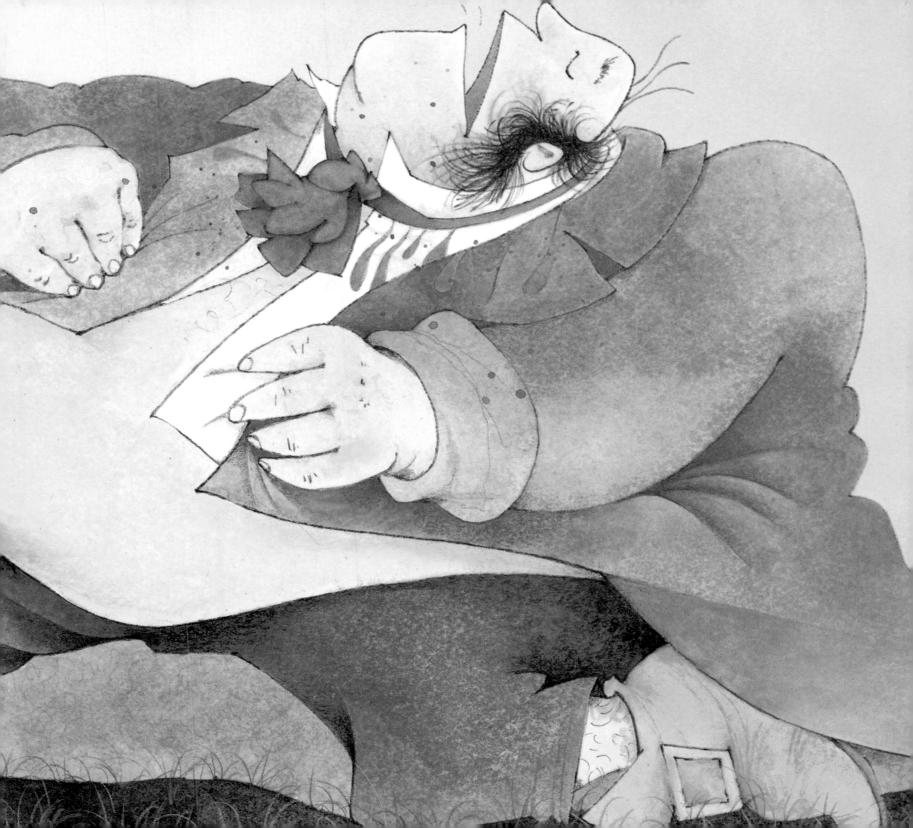

The giant was clutching his belly and had turned a terrible shade of green. Jack whispered in the harp's ear. The harp began to sing:

Fee-fi-fiddledy-dee.
You'll not get the gold, the hen, or me.
Jack is too nimble, he's just too quick.
Watch him run, lickety-split!

And with that, Jack took off like a shot.

The giant jumped to his feet screaming, "Come back here, you!" but quickly doubled over in pain. It looked like Jack was going to make a clean getaway, just like he'd cleverly planned.

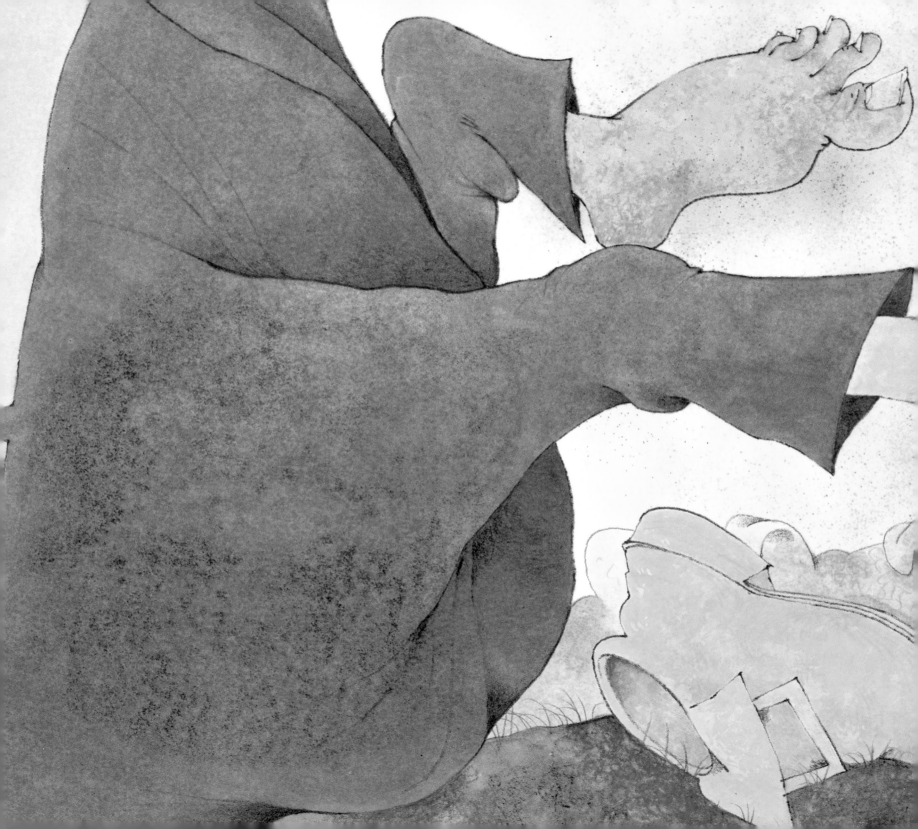

Until the giant, who was not quite as stupid as Jack had thought, pulled a trick of his own. He kicked off his boots and waved his smelly old toes in the air.

Imagine the stinkiest feet ever...then imagine ten thousand more. One whiff and a flock of geese fainted in midair. Trees keeled over like wilted lettuce. Why, even the clouds in the sky took off for Canada, the smell was so bad.

Jack couldn't handle it, either. He became dizzy, his knees buckled under him, and he

fell
to
the
ground.

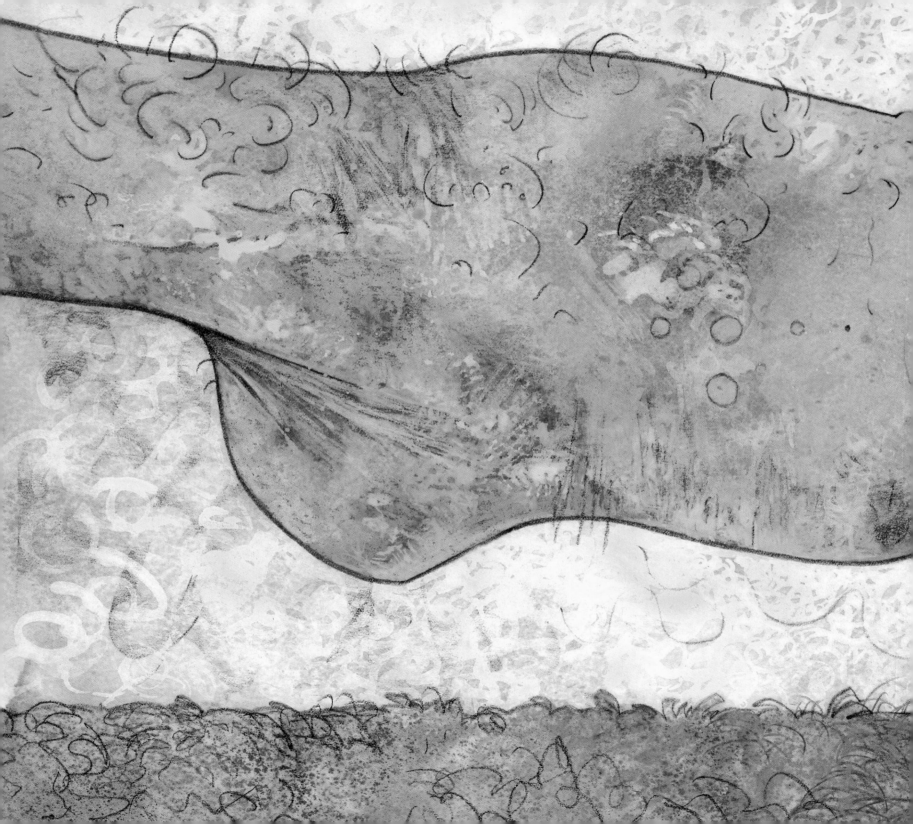

And so this story might have tragically ended—
with Jack spread with mustard and eaten on toast,
and the coins and the hen and the magic harp back
in Giantland—if Jack hadn't been such a quick
thinker. Gasping for breath, he crawled to his roses
and breathed deeply. So fragrant were they that he
instantly revived and escaped down the mountain
with all the loot.

Whew!

The giant became madder than a rained-on rooster. In a tantrum, he stomped his feet so hard the vibrations went all the way to California (where some folks say they are shaking things up still). He stomped again and again, harder and harder, until the jolts were so powerful that the top of the mountain fell in, swallowing him and his stinky tootsies, too.

There he stays to this very day.

To Kelsey, the soul of an artist
T. B.

To Mark, who can always make me guffaw
W. H.

Text copyright © 2001 by Tom Birdseye
Illustrations copyright © 2001 by Will Hillenbrand
All Rights Reserved
Printed in the United States of America
www.holidayhouse.com
The artwork for this book was prepared on 100% cotton vellum.
The artist tinted both the front and back surfaces of the paper with a variety of media,
including woodless pencils, inks, egg tempera, colored pencils, water-soluble crayon, and oils.
The art was then drymounted on bristol board.

Library of Congress Cataloging-in-Publication Data
Birdseye, Tom.
Look Out, Jack! The giant is back / by Tom Birdseye; illustrated by JWill Hillenbrand.—1st ed.
p. cm.
Summary: Taking up where "Jack and the Beanstalk" left off, the felled giants big brother comes after Jack,
but once again Jack's quick mind gets him out of trouble in the nick of time.
ISBN 0-8234-1450-7 (hardcover)   ISBN 0-8234-1776-X (paperback)
[1. Fairy tales 2. Giants—Fiction.] I. Hillenbrand, Will, ill. II. Title.
PZ8.B535 Lo 2001
[E] 00-032006

And Jack? Why, he's back on his farm with his mama, gathering golden eggs, listening to that magic harp, and growing the prettiest, most fragrant roses you can imagine. He'll get married soon, I reckon, and live happily ever after.

Because this time that really is—THE END of the story.

Wham blam hickity hack!
No more giants to bother Jack!
He now be living a life of ease
Sitting on the front porch, pretty as you please!